brush
A TALE OF TWO FOXES

PIERCE FEIRITEAR has written many books for children including *Return To Troy* and the zany *Brainstorm* series. His other books include *The King's Secret*, *How Cuchulainn Got His Name*, and *The Irish Famine* which he co-wrote with Gail Seekamp. He works as a teacher and taught this book's illustrator, Conor O Brien, in primary school. Pierce lives in Dublin with his wife Gail and family.

CONOR O BRIEN is fourteen years old and lives in Drumcondra, Dublin. He has two brothers and a sister. He started drawing when he was four years old and has not stopped since (as Mr. Feiritear discovered back in 3rd class!). He has won many art competitions (including Energy Saving sponsored by the ESB, in 1998). Conor is a student at C.U.S. in Leeson Street.

PIERCE FEIRITEAR

brush
A TALE OF TWO FOXES

Illustrated by
Conor O Brien

PIXIE BOOKS

First published in 2002 by Pixie Books
72 Cabra Park, Phibsboro, Dublin 7, Ireland.

Reprinted 2004, 2006

Text copyright © 2002 Pierce Feiritear
Illustrations copyright © 2002 Conor O Brien

ISBN 0-9543544-0-0

Editor: Gail Seekamp
Typesetting: Keystrokes
Cover illustration: Conor O Brien
Cover design: Jason Ellams
Printed in Ireland by Colour Books

1 I Freeze, You Freeze

One Christmas Eve, when the snow swirled and the wind howled, a crow swooped over the rooftops of Clonowen village. The bird was in a hurry for she carried a large piece of bread. She flew over the village square, where laughing children played, across the river and the white fields towards the woods on a hill in the distance. Then, after circling the trees, she came down on the branch of an old oak.

She was about to eat the bread when she saw a fox staring up at her.

Go on, drop it, please drop it, the fox was thinking.

The crow was no fool. She had searched all day for this food and was not going to let even a crumb fall. But she could not eat with a fox staring at her like that.

So, with a noisy flap of her wings she flew away.

The fox lowered his head and stepped back into his den, which was at the foot of the tree. His two cubs now stared at him.

"I'm hungry, Dad," said Misty.

"We haven't eaten in two days," said Ash, her brother.

"Your father and I know that," said Mother Fox, who was sitting next to her cubs. "We know."

"And it's Christmas Eve," added Misty, miserably.

Mother Fox and Father Fox looked at each other.

"Well, we can't just sit here and starve," said Father Fox. "Let's go out."

"Good ol' Dad," cheered the young foxes.

"But there's a snowstorm," protested Mother Fox.

"We've no choice," Father Fox replied.

A few moments later, Father Fox and Mother Fox and their two cubs stepped out into the woods. The little foxes were almost up to their noses in snow.

"It's fr-ee-ee-zing," said Misty.

Ash stared at the sky in wonder. "Wow, look at those flakes flying everywhere!"

"Tricksters, pay attention," ordered Father Fox.

"Yes, line up behind your dad," said Mother Fox.

The cubs did as they were told.

"Good," said Father Fox. "I want you to stay like that. Me in front, your mother behind. All in one line. No wandering off anywhere. Understand?"

"Yes, Dad, we understand," answered both.

"And watch me, okay? If I freeze, you freeze!"

"But we're already freezing," said Ash.

"You know what I mean, Ash. If I stop dead-still, you do it. Is that clear?"

Both nodded.

"But if I say 'scatter', what do you do?"

"We scatter," said Misty, giggling.

"Yes," said their father. "We scatter like a...like a..."

"Like a bunch of scared rabbits," prompted Mother Fox.

"Yes, like rabbits," said Father Fox. "And we meet back here."

"But that's only if there's danger," Mother Fox told her cubs.

"Correct. There's no need to worry," added their father.

"Do you think we will catch a rabbit this time, Dad?" asked Ash.

"I hope so," said Father Fox.

"Yes!" shouted Misty. "Rabbit pie for dinner!"

"Sh-sh-sh, you'll give us away," said Mother Fox.

"Your mother is right," said Father Fox. "Now, let's get a move on." He turned and with one leap he set off through the snow.

"Wait for us, Dad," called Misty and Ash, bounding along behind as best they could.

Behind them, keeping a watchful eye, came Mother Fox.

The hungry foxes searched everywhere but there were no rabbits to be seen in the woods. There were no squirrels either. Or mice. Or birds. Not a single

one. Not even a print left by one. Foxes, it seemed, were the only animals out in this snowstorm.

Father Fox came to a halt. It was dark by now, yet the snow gleamed in the moonlight. He stood there, unsure of what to do next.

"Do you see something Dad?" whispered Misty.

"Smell a rabbit?" whispered Ash.

"Your dad is thinking, that's all," said Mother Fox.

"Well, I'm hungry," complained Ash.

"My belly's rumbling," groaned Misty, "and I'm tired."

"Shush now, we'll think of something," said their mother. "Perhaps we should try digging for worms?" she suggested.

Misty and Ash usually turned their noses up at worms but now they seemed quite inviting.

"No," said Father Fox. "The ground is frozen hard. It's a waste of time digging for the wriggly fellows .... No, there's only one place left to go."

"And where is that?" asked Mother Fox.

Father Fox stared at her.

"Surely you're not thinking of...are you?" said she.

"Yes," he replied.

2 The MacLugs

Mother Fox whispered, so the cubs couldn't hear: "We can't bring them over to the MacLugs' farm. It's too dangerous."

"I won't put the cubs in danger, I promise. I'll go in myself," said Father Fox.

"I don't want you going in there either. Are you gone mad or something? Think of that hound. Remember what he did to Grandpa..."

"I know dear, and I'm sorry about that. But your father took big risks - like going into a hen-house in broad daylight. The hound is well locked up by now."

"What about the MacLugs?"

"What about them? I'll just snoop around that's all."

"Dad, Mam, what are we doing?" Misty interrupted.

"What are you talking about?" asked Ash.

"One moment," said their mother. "Your father and I are discussing something."

"We know that," Misty muttered under her breath.

"Guess what Misty?" said her brother.

"What?"

"You're gone all white with the snow."

"So are you."

"You look funny."

"Not as funny as you. But I'm not cold now, are you?"

"Nah. I'm just STARVING, that's all."

"Me too. I could eat a hedgehog."

"No, you couldn't."

"Could so."

"Not a hedgehog, you couldn't."

"I'd eat anything right now. Even an onion." Misty turned to her Mam and Dad. "Will you please...!"

"All right, tricksters, I've got a plan," declared Father Fox.

"Take no chances, remember," Mother Fox whispered in his ear.

"We've had no luck here, so we're going over to the MacLugs' place," said Father Fox.

"For the chickens?" the little foxes asked.

"Yes, for the chickens."

"Hurray!" cried Misty and Ash. "Chicken for dinner!"

"We might even grab a turkey while we're at it,"

said their father. "It is Christmas, after all."

"Good ol' Dad," cheered the two cubs.

"But we'll have to be very careful near the MacLugs' house," Mother Fox warned.

"Now, line up again, tricksters, and follow me," said Father Fox.

And away he marched with a "Hup, two, three, four.... Hup, two, three, four...."

So the foxes left the woods behind and headed across the white and silent fields.

Before long they came to the lane that led to the MacLugs' place. The lights were on in the house.

"Wait here, I'll be back in a jiffy," said Father Fox.

"Remember what I said: don't take any chances," warned Mother Fox.

"I promise."

Ash and Misty watched their father disappear into the darkness.

I wish I had some food, thought Misty, her mouth watering. *Chicken or turkey, duckling or lamb, beef or bacon...*

I'd love some roast turkey, thought Ash, his tummy rumbling. *Or chicken burgers, steak, ham, pork chops...and especially, sausages!*

Father Fox entered the yard and stopped. The

farmhouse was right in front of him. Inside, one of the MacLug brothers sat at a table.

Slicer MacLug was a small, scrawny man who wore a thin moustache and an eye-patch. His one piercing blue eye missed little in the world. At this moment, that eye was focused on a pile of coins and notes on the table. Slicer MacLug was counting his money.

Good, that will keep him busy, thought the fox. No, it was not Slicer MacLug he was worried about. Or his brother, Smudge, who ran the butcher shop in the village. It was the hound that bothered him.

Anyway, I'm sure he's locked up and asleep by now, thought Father Fox. *If I can just slip past his kennel, grab a chicken and make a dash for it...*

He ran across the yard towards the outhouses. Little did he know that the MacLugs' hound was watching him from behind the bars of his kennel.

Slowly, Raptor crouched, his yellow eyes fixed on the fox. If that fox came close enough, he would grab hold of him through the bars...

Father Fox came to the first outhouse, on the corner. *Only the kennel between me and the hen-house,* he thought. *Easy does it...*

Raptor's brown hair bristled. His nostrils quivered. He bared his deadly fangs. Still, he held himself back.

Down the lane, Mother Fox and her two cubs waited and waited. The wind had died down but the snow was still falling.

Suddenly there was an explosion of noise from the farmyard.

"It's the hound!" gasped Mother Fox.

"Oh-oh," said the cubs.

Just then, Father Fox shot out of the dark like a bullet. "Scatter!" he screamed. "Scatter!"

The foxes flew down the lane.

Turning the corner, they were caught in the dazzling headlights of a *MacLug Meats* van. Smudge MacLug swerved, not to avoid the foxes but to try and run them down. Instantly the foxes leapt over the wall. The van skidded off the road and into the ditch.

"Cowdung!" roared Smudge, smashing a big hairy fist on the dashboard. He climbed out of the van, threw his woollen cap on the ground and stamped on it with his hobnailed boots.

A few seconds later, his brother came running down the lane with a shotgun.

"It's too late, they've gone, Captain," said Smudge.

"Who are they?" Slicer asked in his squeaky voice.

"Foxes."

"The vermin! I should have let Raptor loose."

"And look what they've done to my van!" roared Smudge, slamming the door almost off its hinges.

"Don't worry, my dear brother, we'll take care of your van," said Slicer, wiping the snow from his dark and expensive suit (the same suit he wore every day of the year).

Smudge was still fuming. "And then what?"

"Then we'll take care of the foxes," said Slicer, his one blue eye gleaming.

3 Another Plan

"Look, scatter means scatter. You shouldn't have followed me," said Father Fox, trying to catch his breath. He and the two cubs were huddled together under a bush, a few fields away.

"Where's Mam?" whispered Ash.

"Probably making her own way back home," panted Father Fox. "That was the plan."

"No, there she is!" exclaimed Misty. "Psst, Mam, Mam..."

The ghostly figure of Mother Fox glided towards them. "It's okay, they're not chasing us," said their mother.

"Thank heavens for that," sighed Father Fox.

Mother Fox stared at him. "Dear me, what happened to you?"

"Look, Dad, look at your fur," gasped Misty.

"What?" Their father turned to examine himself.

"A big lump of it's missing," cried Ash.

"On your backside!" said Misty.

Father Fox looked at the big bald patch. "Funny, I didn't feel a thing," said he, suddenly noticing the cold on his bare skin.

"Poor dear, did the hound get hold of you?" asked Mother Fox.

"It's all a blur to me, it happened so quickly," he said. "Still, could be worse - it's just a piece of fur. What matters is we're safe."

"I'm still hungry," Ash reminded him.

"What are we going to do?" asked Misty.

"Well, we've come this far, we're going to have to keep searching," said Mother Fox. "We'll go to the village and look for food there."

"Oh, no, not the rubbish bins," cried the children. "We don't want to eat rubbish. It's Christmas!"

"I never said we'd have to eat rubbish," answered their mother.

"But that's what Dad brought back last time he went to the village," said Misty.

"Yeah, rubbish," Ash agreed. "Half a burger with horrible ketchup, yuck!"

"And three-day-old chicken wings from the takeaway on the corner," added Misty sourly.

"Well, I'm sorry, tricksters," said Father Fox. "We're going to the village."

"Why?"

"That's the 'why'," their father answered crossly. "And if we have to search the bins, then we will -

and that's all there is to it. Foxes have to do that sometimes."

"But Dad!"

"No 'buts'," said Father Fox. "Now, let's get a move on."

"Misty, Ash, please do what your father says," said Mother Fox in a soft voice. She felt sorry for her cubs.

There were no cars on the road because of the snow and the foxes moved freely. Before long the twinkling lights of the village of Clonowen came into view down in the valley.

"Be on your guard," warned Father Fox. "And watch your back. There's danger at every turn down there."

Ash and Misty felt a tingle of excitement. They had never been allowed to go to the village before.

"Maybe we won't have to do the bins after all," whispered Ash.

"Yeah," said Misty. "We might get lucky and find a turkey, a big, fat, juicy, Christmas turkey - with loads of stuffing."

"And we might get some pudding too," said Ash. "With lots of cream on top."

Presently they came to a dark corner on the village square. The square was deserted and blanketed in snow. The only sound was the distant drumming of the Clonowen waterfall.

In the middle of the square stood a giant Christmas tree. Its red, green and blue fairy lights flickered on and off, casting their colours on the snow.

Close to the tree was a big snowman, which the children had made. Its hat had fallen off and was slowly filling with snow.

"Good, the coast is clear. Spread out and see what you can find," said Father Fox. "We'll meet back here."

"Remember what you've been taught," said Mother Fox, turning to her cubs. "Follow your nose. Stick close to the walls. Keep moving. And don't take any...?"

"Chances," Misty and Ash chirped.

Mother Fox gave them a kind look. "Yes, now, off you go, and stay together."

Misty and Ash slipped away into the shadows. They headed towards a row of cottages a short distance away.

"Follow me," whispered Misty as she turned into one of the gardens. "I think I smell something nice."

"I smell it too," said her brother.

They crossed the garden of Number 4, slipped

through a fence into Number 6 and then hopped over a low stone wall into the next garden. The delicious smell came from Number 8.

Ash and Misty followed their noses right up to the window of the cottage. They put their paws on the window-sill and peered inside.

"Take a look at that," gasped Ash.

On a table was the most glorious food a fox could ever have imagined. First to catch the eye was a huge turkey, stuffed and ready for the oven. Beside that was a mouth-watering ham. On the next plate, a pudding. Next to that, a trifle. Then some mince pies.... Not to mention the Christmas cake.

"This is torture," cried Ash and he began scratching at the window-pane.

"Stop it," Misty ordered. "You'll give us away." She could see there was no way of getting near that food. "Come on, let's move."

Poor Ash dragged himself away from the window.

They left the cottages and crossed over to the shops.

All the shutters were down, except for the one shop: *MacLug Meats.*

"Ah, this is just too much," said Misty looking up at the shop window. High on the right hung a row of plucked turkeys. Over on the left, on the shelves, were dozens of chickens - dozens of them! But what was really cruel was the sight of the trays of meat right there in front of their noses, behind the glass.

"Sirloin steak," sighed Misty.

"Fillet steak," sighed Ash.

"Leg of lamb."

"Lamb chops."

"Pork."

"Pot Roast Beef."

"Liver."

"And s-s-sausages." Ash tried not to cry. "My favourites!"

The two little foxes stood and stared. It was all so unfair.

And they would have stood and stared for longer but for the sound of a sharp yelp from across the square.

"Listen, it's Mam calling us," said Misty.

"Where is she?" asked her brother.

"Over there."

Ash looked and saw his mother standing in the doorway of the *Horse and Hound Tavern*. "And where's Dad?"

"I'll give you one guess."

"Oh no," groaned Ash. He looked towards the *Golden Boat Takeaway* and spied the dim figure of a fox rooting in a rubbish bin. "I'm not going over there," he complained. "I'm not going to eat rubbish for Christmas. I'm just not!"

"Calm down, calm down," said Misty.

"I don't care what anyone says, I'm not eating rotten chicken wings."

Misty glanced towards the tall, red-bricked houses nearby. "Come on, let's try some of those houses before we go. We might get lucky."

"We'd better get lucky because this is not funny."

They moved towards the houses of Hillside Terrace, little knowing that someone in the corner house was watching them.

4 Katie

Like all the other children in the village that night, Katie found it hard to sleep. She had tossed and turned, and turned and tossed. She even counted sheep, 114 of them. But it was no use.

I wonder what'll be under the Christmas tree tomorrow? she thought over and over.

Last year it was a bike. This year she had asked for a surprise.

What'll it be? What'll it be? thought Katie. Not knowing was driving her mad.

Maybe I should count sheep again. Up to 300 this time, she told herself. She closed her eyes and pictured some sheep. She began counting:

One sheep, two sheep, three, four, five sheep...

She stopped counting on sheep number 57. Counting them was easy. The problem was that instead of jumping over a fence one by one, the silly animals ran around together doing crazy things like cartwheels and leap-frogs (if that's the right word). Why, one of them even lay down on its back laughing, paddling its feet in the air!

"This is no use," said Katie out loud. She opened her eyes and stared at the ceiling again.

I wonder is it snowing still? I can't hear any sound on the window-pane. Mam said it would be a white Christmas. But what if it's all gone in the morning? And what about that snowman we made in the square?

This last thought was too much for her. She pulled back the blankets and jumped out of bed.

"It is SO cold."

She stepped over to the window and peeped out. And that was when Mother Fox let out her yelp.

Immediately Katie looked towards the *Horse and Hound Tavern* and the *Golden Boat Takeaway.*

It's a fox. At the bins. It must be very hungry, she thought. *Oh look, there's two more over at the shops. They're little ones. Poor things. Hey, they're coming this way...*

With that she hurried from the room. Quiet as a mouse, she tip-toed down the stairs, rushed into the kitchen and switched on the light. Her teeth were chattering as she opened a tin of biscuits. She counted them out on a plate: "Three chocolate ones...two pink wafer ones...one creamy one with a red heart...and three crispy shortbread ones. Let me see...three foxes...?" She did a quick sum in her head. "That's three each."

The front gardens on Hillside Terrace were very small, with barely enough room for a flower-bed.

Ash and Misty had come as far as the gate of Katie's house when they heard the door opening.

They pulled back behind the hedge.

"Freeze," whispered Misty.

Light spilled out onto the path.

They heard the clink of a plate being put on the ground. Then came the sound of the door closing.

"Can you smell what I smell?" whispered Misty.

"I sure can," said Ash, his face brightening. "I think they left something out for us."

"What if it's a trap?"

"It's not a trap." Ash remembered his mother and father saying that not all people were bad like the MacLugs. Some people liked foxes and even left food out for them.

The two foxes waited a moment, glancing around.

"Are you ready?" whispered Ash, eager to grab the food.

"Wait," said Misty. "What's that noise?"

"That's just the waterfall," answered Ash.

"No, it's something else," said Misty. "Listen."

Ash cocked an ear and heard a rumbling sound coming up the hill at the back of the houses. "Don't worry about the noise," he said. "I'm going in for the food."

"Wait, wait," said Misty. The rumble was growing louder and louder.

"Come on, let's get the food," urged her brother. He stuck his head out from the hedge and saw the plate of biscuits. "Wow, Misty, look at this!"

The rumble swelled to a roar, so loud now that Misty had to shout: "Leave it. Come on!"

"No."

As Ash made a dive for the biscuits, a monster of a machine swung around the corner. The ground shook.

"Scatter!" Misty screamed, but she could not be heard.

Ash snatched two biscuits (the chocolate ones). He scurried out the gate and almost ran under the gigantic wheels of a snow plough.

5 Poor Dad

"Ooooooh...whoooooh," groaned Father Fox on Christmas morning. "I'm as sick as a dog!"

"You poor fellow," said Mother Fox.

"Look, Dad, your tummy's very big," said Misty.

"It's huge," agreed Ash. "You must have eaten a lot of that rubb... I mean, takeaway food."

"It's not huge," said Mother Fox. "Your father's tummy is swollen, that's all."

Father Fox tried to get up off the ground, but his legs felt like water. "Ooooooh...whoooooh, I think I'm going to get sick again," he moaned.

"Lie down dear, lie down and you'll feel better," said Mother Fox.

Father Fox fell in a heap on the ground again.

"Poor Dad," said Misty and Ash, snuggling up close to their father.

"It's those spare ribs," said Mother Fox. "They made you sick."

"You don't have to tell me. That's the last bin I'll ever eat from."

"Did you have any of those chicken wings, Dad?"

Ash asked. "They'd poison a dead rat!"

"Please, please, stop talking about food," cried Father Fox. "And dead rats!"

Mother Fox took her cubs to one side. "I want you to stay here and look after your dad. I'm going out to hunt."

"Okay, Mam," said Misty.

"Please bring us back something to eat," said Ash. "It's been three days!"

"I know," said their mother. "I know."

Two hours later, a glum Mother Fox returned to the den. "I'm sorry, little ones, I've nothing for you," she told them.

Misty and Ash hung their heads.

"But the snow is beginning to thaw," added Mother Fox, trying to sound cheerful. "I'm sure there'll be lots of rabbits and mice running about tomorrow."

"Tomorrow?" cried Ash. "I can't wait till tomorrow."

Misty looked at her mother. "Mam, will you let me and Ash go out?"

"Yes, good idea," yelped her brother.

"I told you, there's nothing out there."

"We might get lucky," said Misty.

"Please, Mam, please," begged Ash.

Mother Fox did not know what to say.

"Let them out," came the weak voice of Father Fox. "They're big enough now."

"Dad's right," said Misty.

Mother Fox sighed. "Very well, just this once," she said. "But don't go out of the woods."

"Hurray!" cheered the two cubs. "Let's go hunting."

And hunt they did.

The trouble was, there was no food in the woods. NO FOOD.

"This is a waste of time," said Misty, finally.

"What do you want to do?"

"Go back, I suppose."

Ash shook his head. "I'm not going back until I get something to eat."

"Okay, but where?"

Ash thought for a moment. "I say we go to the MacLugs' place."

"No," said Misty. "I'm not going anywhere near that hound."

"Right, we'll go to the village then."

Misty shook her head. "Mam said-"

"Listen to me. Mam won't mind when we bring

back the food, will she?"

"You won't find any food in the village."

"That's not true. There's lots of food if you know the right place. Remember the biscuits?"

"Biscuit," said Misty. "We got just one biscuit."

"Two. I dropped the other one," said Ash. "Anyway, that's not the point. The point is, there's lots more where they came from."

"Do you think so?"

"I know so."

Hunger was winning the argument.

"And today is Christmas Day," added Ash. "Think of all the food they'll put on that plate for us. Turkey, ham, roast potatoes! Will you come with me?"

"Okay, I'm with you."

"Come on the foxes!" cheered Ash.

6   The Sausage Snake

It was midday in Clonowen and in every kitchen Christmas dinner was being prepared. The smell of roast turkey wafted around the square.

Katie and her friends were playing in the snow. They threw snowballs, trying to knock the hat off the snowman's head.

Not far away, by the corner under a hedge, the two foxes lay waiting.

"That smell is driving me wild," whispered Ash.

"Why should they have all that food while we starve?" said Misty angrily.

"Don't worry. We won't starve for much longer," answered her brother.

Misty peeped out at the children. "I wish they'd move away."

Her wish was answered a moment later when the children began playing 'Chase' and ran to the other side of the square.

"Okay, let's go," said Ash.

Just as the night before, they headed for the row of cottages nearby. They crossed the garden of

Number 4, slipped through a fence into Number 6 and hopped over a low stone wall into the next garden. Here, they crouched by the gate.

"There's the 'biscuit' house over there," said Ash, looking across the square to Hillside Terrace.

"Look, the door's opening."

They watched as a woman walked out of the corner house and called to one of the children. Then they saw a girl walking towards the house.

The foxes waited. Katie walked into her house and closed the door behind her.

"Do you think the biscuits will still be there?" asked Misty.

"Wait, take a look over there," answered her brother, turning towards the shops.

The door of *MacLug Meats* was open.

"Wow," gasped Misty. "Will we take a closer look?"

"Heh, heh, we'll take more than a closer look," joked Ash. "Come on, follow me."

Smudge MacLug looked at the clock on the wall. It said 12.07. It was time to close up the shop. "Will you hurry up, Boss," he called out to his brother, as he slapped down a pile of sausages on the counter.

They were special sausages he had made for the Christmas dinner. "I can't wait to tuck into these."

A moment later, Slicer appeared from the back of the shop. He placed a leg of lamb beside the sausages. "Who needs turkey when you can have food like this!"

"Let's lock up and go home," said Smudge, pulling on his woollen cap.

"Your wish is my command," said Slicer. "Now, where did I put those keys?"

"Don't tell me you've lost the stinkin' keys," groaned Smudge.

"Patience, dear boy, patience," said Slicer. "And watch your tongue...or I'll have to cut it out."

Ash crept up to the door and took one peep in. He saw Slicer MacLug rummaging in one of the drawers and Smudge with his back to the counter. And on the counter he saw...(well, you know what he saw).

The crafty fox had one chance and he meant to take it.

"I'll get the lamb. You go for the sausages," he whispered to Misty.

"Are you sure?"

But Ash had already gone in through the door.

Oh-oh, we're in trouble now, thought Misty. She

felt her legs go weak. Her heart started pounding like a drum. Still, she went in after her brother.

"Ah, here they are," said Slicer holding up the keys.

"Right, Boss, let's mosey," said Smudge, turning to go. Suddenly he froze. The lamb had vanished from the counter. And, right before his eyes, the pile of sausages was uncoiling like a snake.

"What the blazes!" roared Smudge. He made a dive for the sausages but they were gone. The sausage-snake was now sliding out the door.

"Thieves!" bellowed Smudge. "Thieves!"

He grabbed a brush and leapt over the counter. Slicer came behind him with a gigantic knife.

Away went the foxes, Ash with the lamb and Misty with the sausages.

Slicer ran out the door and hurled the knife at them. It missed by a mile and smacked onto the snow.

Smudge threw away his brush and waved a fist in the air. "I'll get you foxes," he shouted after them. "I'll get you for this."

Over in her house, Katie heard the racket. She stood at the window, laughing as the foxes raced across the square with the string of sausages trailing behind them. Then they disappeared.

7 Christmas Dinners

"How many sausages have you had Misty?"

Misty let out a big burp and laughed. "I don't know. I've lost count."

"This is my seventh," said Ash.

"Seven? That's enough," said Mother Fox. "You'll get sick like your dad."

The young foxes glanced at their father still curled up asleep in the corner of the den.

"Poor Dad, he's not better yet," said Misty.

"Still, we'd better keep some sausages for him. He'll be hungry soon enough," said Ash.

"That's right, now put them away," said their mother. "I've something to say to you."

"Yes Mam?"

The two foxes stopped eating and looked up at their mother, who looked down at them.

"You should not have gone to the village by yourselves. You had no permission to do that," she told them. "You are not to do that again."

"We won't, Mam," said the cubs.

Then Mother Fox looked down at the food her

cubs had brought home and she smiled. "But I have to say...you've done a great job."

"Thank you, Mam," said Ash and Misty, their hearts swelling with pride.

"We're big foxes now, aren't we?" said Misty.

"Well, nearly," said their mother.

"You should have seen the MacLugs," said Ash. "They were...they were like-"

"Like dogs," said Misty.

"Yeah, like wild dogs," said Ash. "Roaring and shouting and screaming and bawling."

"And on Christmas Day," added Misty.

"One of them even threw a knife at us," said Ash.

"Disgraceful," said Mother Fox, horrified.

"All because we took a little bit of meat," said Misty.

"And they have a shop full of it," said Ash.

"I think we should go back for more - that'll teach them," said Misty

"No, you will NOT go back for more," insisted their mother. "Those MacLugs are dangerous. You're lucky the hound wasn't with them. You would have been finished."

Ash and Misty looked at each other and fell quiet.

Across the fields at that very moment, the MacLugs' hound was crunching a huge bone in his masters' kitchen. Christmas Day was the one day in the year they let him inside. Raptor was happy.

But his masters were fuming. They had eaten fried eggs and mashed potatoes for dinner.

"No sausages or lamb. Our Christmas dinner was ruined," snarled Smudge.

"By foxes!" added Slicer.

"When do we go a-huntin' 'em?" asked his brother.

"Just as soon as that snow clears. It will be gone in a day or two."

"The sooner the better," Smudge added.

"It won't be hard to find that vermin in the woods."

"We'll wipe out the lot of them."

"And then we'll chop them up," said Slicer.

"And mince them," said Smudge.

Slicer began to laugh evilly. "We'll turn them into burgers and sell them."

"Yeah, fox burgers," said Smudge, grinning.

"And no-one in the village will ever know, dear boy," said Slicer, his blue eye glinting.

8   Out Hunting

On the day after St. Stephen's Day, Father Fox woke up feeling a little better.

"Would you like some sausage, dear?" enquired Mother Fox

"Just a small bit," said Father Fox, and he rose unsteadily to his feet.

"Lie back down, I'll bring it to you," said Mother Fox.

He did as he was told. "On second thoughts, I think I'll wait a while before I eat," said he.

"That's wise," said Mother Fox. "You're still very weak."

"Poor Dad," said Misty.

"But at least he's on the mend," said Mother Fox. "By the way, where's Ash?"

"He's out hunting," answered Misty. "The snow's almost gone and the rabbits are out again."

"That's my son, looking after the family while his dad's ill," said Father Fox proudly.

"I've been hunting too, Dad," said Misty, a bit miffed. "I brought back those sausages remember?"

"Of course you did, my little treasure," said her dad, "and I'm going to eat one just as soon as my tummy is up to it."

"Well, if your son is out hunting, I hope he hasn't..." Mother Fox stopped in mid-sentence, for she heard a scramble of paws outside the den. "Here he comes now. Looks like he's in a hurry too."

Mother Fox never spoke a truer word. Ash came rushing into the den. His eyes were wild with fear. "The MacLugs are coming!" he gasped.

"Where?" asked his mother.

"This way. Get out of here quick."

"Wait. Is the hound with them?"

"Yes and lots of other dogs. Hurry up!" Ash turned to his father. "Dad, get up will you?"

"I haven't the strength to go anywhere," sighed Father Fox.

His family looked at him and they knew it was true.

"You'll have to go without me," he added.

Just then the sound of yelping rose from somewhere outside. Ash, shaking like a leaf, stared at his mother. "What'll we do Mam?"

"The pair of you go. I'm staying with your father," she replied.

"But Mam-"

"Go! Now!" she snapped. "While there's still time!"

Ash and Misty hesitated.

"Do I have to push you out!" snarled their mother, more cross than they had ever seen her.

Ash and Misty did what they were told and left.

First, they poked their heads out of the den, looking this way and that. The baying of hounds, many hounds, filled the air.

"We can't just run away and leave Mam and Dad," said Misty.

"I know. It's all our fault," said Ash. "But what can we do?"

"There's only one thing we can do."

"What's that?"

"You know," said Misty. "Come with me."

9 Tally Ho!

In a clearing in the woods sat three riders on their horses: Slicer, Smudge and their aunt, Polly MacLug.

Polly was a giant of a woman with a broad, freckled face and a big mop of red curly hair. Everyone called her Polly the Builder, for she had built many houses in Clonowen over the years. She also ran the biggest farm in the area, and was Master of the Clonowen Hunt. Dressed in a blood-red hunting jacket, she had brought twenty hounds with her. They were milling around the horses' heels, sniffing and yapping, and yapping and sniffing.

"Look at them runnin' around in circles," roared Smudge. "Spread out, spread out you silly mutts."

"They are foxhounds, not mutts, lad," Polly corrected him. "And they're experts at this. They'll smell out those foxes any moment - long before that mad hound of yours will," she added, throwing a look at Raptor.

"Our dog may not have the nose but he has the legs - and teeth. Just you wait and see," Smudge answered with a chuckle.

"Auntie, you'd better mind what you say about Raptor," put in Slicer. "He understands every word."

"You're joking," said Aunt Polly, turning in her saddle only to find the hound's yellow eyes staring right at her.

Then something else caught her eye. She could hardly believe it. A pair of young foxes darted from the trees in full view of the pack.

All hell broke loose.

The hounds scrambled to the chase as if a bolt of electricity had shot through them.

"We're off!" shouted Polly, spurring her horse forward.

"Tally Ho!" roared Slicer.

"Yee-haw!" screamed Smudge.

Misty and Ash moved like the wind, leaving the pack behind. Past trees, under bushes, over logs and boulders they flew. They knew every inch of the woods.

Misty led the way. She was as fresh as a daisy, unlike her brother who had hunted earlier. He was already dropping back. "Keep up," she told him. She knew they would need a good lead before they broke out from the woods.

Coming to the stream, she slowed down. "Follow me. Do every thing I do, okay?"

Ash knew what she meant. Each time their dad brought them to this stream, he'd stop and say: "Remember, tricksters, water is a fox's best friend. It takes no prints and holds no scent. If you're really in trouble, head for water."

Into the freezing stream they leapt. They trotted upstream for a bit, then left the water, zig-zagged

46

through the trees and circled back to the stream.

"This'll really tie them in knots," said Misty, dashing through the water again.

"They'll be running in circles," said Ash gleefully.

For the second time, the foxes left the water and ran a merry dance through the trees.

"Now, for the best part," said Misty. "The jungle."

"Yes!" cheered Ash. "That'll really slow them up."

What Misty called the 'jungle' was the big clump of rhododendrons at the far end of the woods. Here, the bushes were so dense that no horse could pass through. Even the foxhounds would find it difficult. But for little foxes who knew the way, it was as easy as pie. They hopped, leaped, wriggled and crawled their way through.

"Listen up," said Misty when they finally came out to the fields. Both of them stopped and cocked their ears.

"They've dropped a long way back," said Misty.

"Those hounds are as thick as bricks," said Ash.

"I know," said Misty. "But we're out in the open now. They won't be long coming."

10 A Bet

The little foxes crossed the fields at a steady trot.

"What's the plan?" Ash asked his sister.

"I don't know yet. Just keep moving."

"Okay, you're the boss," said Ash. "At least Mam and Dad are safe."

"I hope so. Poor Dad wouldn't stand a chance against those hounds."

"I don't mind the hounds so much as the MacLugs' dog. I hate him," said Ash. "After what he did to Grandpa."

"Well, he's not going to get us."

"You bet."

"Now, let's stop talking and start running," said Misty, moving faster.

The ground was soft. All the snow was gone but for a few spots of ice. They crossed some fields and found themselves on the MacLugs' land. Once more, they paused to see if they were being followed.

"No sign of them yet," said Ash.

"They'll be coming soon enough," warned Misty.

"Hey, Misty, do you know what I'm thinking?"

Misty gave her brother a look. "Don't tell me. I don't want to know," she said.

"I'll tell you anyway," said Ash. "I'm thinking: One, the MacLugs are not here. Two, their dog is not here. Three, the chickens ARE here. Four, and so are we!"

"I can't believe my ears," said Misty. "We're being chased by bloodthirsty hounds and you want to stop off for dinner?"

"No, listen to me," said Ash, his eyes a-twinkle. "We just nip up there to the farmhouse, grab a few chickens, hide them and come back for them later. There's plenty of..." Suddenly a hunting-horn sounded.

"What did I tell you?" said Misty, fixing her brother with another look. "Let's get out of here fast!"

They scurried up the MacLugs' lane.

The pack was just four fields away. Polly MacLug's best dog, Snitch, had been first to break out of the woods and pick up the scent. He picked up speed too. Snitch knew he was the leader of the pack. He was fitter, faster than the rest. The foxes had nowhere to hide now. This kill belonged to him.

"That's my boy, Snitch," Polly yelled after him. "Go get them."

Raptor, meanwhile, was loping along at the back

of the pack. He seemed in no hurry. He just moved along at his ease, taking one stride for every two of the others.

"Hey, boys, I see your dog likes to lead from the back," laughed Polly.

"It's a long way from over yet, Auntie," answered Smudge. "Our Raptor is just bidin' his time, that's all."

"Fancy a bet, Aunt Polly?" Slicer called. He loved money and saw a chance to make some.

"Fifty big ones on Snitch," said Polly.

"Fifty on Raptor," said Slicer and with that he smiled and gave his horse another lash of the whip. "Giddy-up, horsey."

11 The Hill

Jumping stone wall after stone wall, the foxes crossed this field and that as they ran for their lives.

Ash and Misty were tiring fast. They could hear the hounds baying for their blood. The sound grew louder and louder.

"They're catching up," cried Ash. "What'll we do?"

Misty did not answer.

"What'll we do, Misty?" Ash's voice was desperate.

"Just keep going. To the top of that hill," urged his sister.

The hill was small, round and steep. Misty ran for it, simply because it was there in front of her. She had no plan. She was just as desperate as her brother.

"There they are - on the hill," shouted Smudge, catching sight of the foxes. "Look at the filthy vermin!"

"Come on, Raptor," snapped Slicer.

Raptor did not need to be told what to do. Not only could he smell the foxes, he could now see them. He surged forward, cutting a path through the pack.

Poor Ash was so tired he could only walk the last few steps to the top of the hill. All he wanted to do was lie down. "I can't go on," he panted.

"You can. Come on!" ordered his sister. She turned and looked back. The hounds were in the field right below them. "They're coming!"

"Some Christmas this is," said Ash.

"Scatter!" screamed Misty. "Scatter!" She sounded just like her dad. That word got Ash moving again. He picked himself up and ran away down the other side of the hill.

But Misty did not move.

She just stood there at the top of the hill.

12 A Trick

Misty watched the hounds and waited. They came in a noisy line. One in the lead, then two more, then the MacLugs' dog followed by the rest of the pack and three riders.

"What's that fox doing?" yelled Slicer.

"Don't ask me," said Polly. She had never seen a fox do this before.

"We have them now," cheered Smudge.

Misty held her breath as they came closer. She saw their open mouths and staring eyes. They were already at the foot of the hill. Still she waited.

Then she moved.

She really moved.

In the wink of an eye, she turned and ran along the top of the hill in full view of the hunt.

Polly realised what the fox was up to. "It's a trick," she shouted.

Most of the hounds followed Misty, but Snitch, Raptor and a few others kept after Ash.

"Snitch, come back," yelled Polly who did not want the pack to split at all costs.

"Come here, Raptor," yelled Smudge.

Snitch was not for turning. Nor was Raptor. They vanished over the top of the hill.

"You silly mutts!" roared Smudge.

Slicer smiled, knowing that Raptor was on the right track. "I'll bring them back, Aunt Polly," he said, not meaning a word of it.

Ash found himself on open ground. There were no bushes, no trees, nowhere to hide. The ground was so soggy, his paws sank into it.

I'm a sitting duck, he thought.

He glanced back, hoping to see Misty. Instead he saw Snitch and Raptor. His heart sank. *I'm done for*, he thought. *Still, I won't give up without a fight.*

By now, Raptor had caught up with Snitch. He gave Polly MacLug's hound a look, as if to say, "So you think you're the best. Well, take a look at this, LOSER!" Then he passed him by, easily.

"Go on, Raptor, my boy, finish him off," Slicer called after him. That fox was 'dead meat'. The money would be his. Maybe he'd put it towards a new shotgun? He thought of all the ducks and pheasants he'd bag with it.

The space between fox and hound closed. Ash felt the great beast bearing down on him. He turned this way, he turned that way, but so did Raptor coming closer and closer.

To his horror, a great brick wall loomed ahead. Ash was trapped.

This is the end, he thought.

Still he kept running, running for the wall.

Then something strange happened. Everything seemed to slow down, like in a dream. His life flashed before his eyes, in pictures:

Ash, curled up close to his mam on the day he was born...

Ash, chewing the meat his dad had brought him...

Ash, rolling and tumbling in the grass with Misty...

Ash chasing a blue butterfly...

Ash staring at falling leaves...

Ash hunting in the snow...

Ash running...running...running...

Suddenly he fell forward and everything went dark.

Am I dead? he thought.

Slicer charged up and jumped off his horse. "Rats' tails!" he spat, throwing down his whip in disgust. The fox had escaped into a pipe which ran through the wall and under a road above.

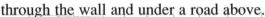

"Leave it, leave it, you ... you baboons!" he screamed at Raptor and Snitch who were snarling and barking at the hole in the wall.

"Come on, let's go back."

Snitch joined him at once.

Raptor, however, had other ideas. He was not a foxhound. He did not obey foxhound rules. Off he went, running down by the wall, looking for a way through.

"We can't go up on the road. Come back, you moron!" screamed Slicer.

But his dog soon found a way. He scrambled up on to the road.

"That's it, one step further and no bone," Slicer threatened. "No bone and no walk - understand? NO WALKIES!"

Raptor was a dog of few words but now, for the first time ever, he fixed his yellow eyes on his master and growled: "I'm not one of the pack. Like it or lump it, MacLug." With that, he trotted across the road.

Slicer was stunned. "What?" His mouth fell open. "What did I just hear?" he squeaked. No, no, he couldn't have heard what he just heard: a dog talking!

"Pull yourself together, man," he told himself.

Shaking his head, he decided to follow his dog.

13 My Misty

As soon as the barking stopped, Ash crawled down the pipe towards the circle of light ahead. It took some time to reach it, for this pipe ran under the main road to Clonowen.

I'm a lucky fox, he thought as he stepped out into the world again.

He took a deep, deep breath.

The sun peeped out from behind the clouds, warming his back. It was as though the sun shone especially for him. How good it felt to be a fox and to be alive.

"I am lucky," said Ash.

A sudden roar startled him. Wheeling around, he saw a huge lorry pass by on the road above. He hurried to the cover of a nearby ditch. Here, he crouched, watchful and alert.

Another sound - a quiet, tinkling sound - came to him. Climbing over the ditch, he found a stream. Water - cold, fresh and clean. How thirsty he was. He started lapping it up.

Ha, ha I showed those hounds, he thought. *I*

showed the MacLugs too. They thought they had me. Well, they were wrong. I out-foxed them. Wait till I tell Dad and Mam. They'll be so proud of me.

At once he was seized with horror. *Misty! My Misty!*

Ash sprang up and away.

Where is she? I've got to find her, I've got to help her.

He crossed ditches and fields, not knowing which way he was going. Ash was in a panic. He had to find his sister, his brave sister who had risked her life for him.

Soon he met a flock of sheep, warm in their woolly winter coats.

"Have you seen another fox around here?" he called out to them. "She was being chased by hounds."

"BAA-AA," answered one.

"BAA-BAAA," answered another. Sheep did not like foxes.

Next, in a ploughed field, he came upon a flock of crows. Some were hopping around searching for seeds (without much success). Others were perched in the bare trees.

"Hey, Crows, have you seen a fox on the run?" he shouted to the ones in the trees.

"CAW, CAW, CAW, CAW," their voices rose up.

"C'mon, tell me," panted Ash.

"CAW, CAW, CAW, CAW, CAW, CAW," came the chorus even louder.

One of the crows dropped off a branch and came swooping down. Ash halted, thinking the bird was about to attack.

"Why should we help you?" asked the crow, whizzing over his head.

"Why not?"

"What have you ever done for us?" said the crow as she turned in the air. "You only try to kill us."

Ash made no reply, for what the crow said was true. Foxes sometimes killed crows. That was the way of things.

The crow winged towards him once more. "If you're looking for the hunt, you're going the wrong way," she said. "Follow the wind and you'll find it."

"Thank you, Missus Crow," said the fox.

"Miss Crow, please," answered the bird, flying away. "I'm Ebony, by the way."

"Thank you, Ebony," said Ash.

So he turned and followed the path of the wind. *I hope that bird's not fooling me*, he thought.

Presently he came to a fallen beech tree lying

across a ditch. It had come down with a mighty crash in the November storm. How strange it looked, with its branches bowed to the ground, while its trunk and roots pointed towards the sky.

I'll climb and take a look, he thought.

He made his way along the trunk and scrambled up the great clump of earth and roots. Away on his left, he could still see the main road. On his right, he saw the gleam of a river and beyond it the rolling hills. In between lay the fields and hedgerows of Clonowen.

He let out three loud barks and waited for an answer.

But for the far-off cawing of crows, all was quiet.

Wait, what was that?

He cocked his ears.

It came again - the faint sound of a hunting horn.

"Oh-oh, here comes double trouble," he said.

What should he do? Run or stay? He remembered what his father once told him: "Hold your nerve. Hold your nerve! To the very last. A fox must learn to do that."

He held on. He even barked again, twice. There was no reply.

Then he caught a flash of red in the distance - it had to be one of the riders.

Next, he heard the baying of hounds. Then the hunting horn, louder now.

Suddenly, out of the corner of his eye, he saw something move in the field below. It was Misty.

14 Cowboys

Ash sprang from the tree. To his surprise, his sister did not seem pleased to see him. "Why all that noise?" she barked.

"I was calling for you."

"I know, but you'll give us away. I heard you the first time."

"Misty, what happened to you?" he gasped, staring at the streak of blood on her back.

"Nothing. Let's make ourselves scarce."

The pair of them skipped through the field.

"After I left you, I ran down the side of the hill," she told him between breaths. "The pack was after me...they were catching up...but I knew what to do. 'Run for the road,' I told myself... Just as I came near it, one of them caught me...but I broke free and got away and onto the road. They had to call the dogs back."

"You're so brave, Misty, and clever too. Does it hurt?"

"I don't feel a thing....What about you? Where did you go?"

"You won't believe it," said her brother. "I came that close - that close - wait till I tell..."

A huge crashing sound cut him short.

A hound had broken through the hedgerow behind them. Ash felt sick when he saw his yellow eyes. It was Raptor, again, followed by Slicer.

The foxes lunged into the ditch.

"Look, Slicer's ambushed them," bellowed Smudge, two fields behind, waving his woollen cap in the air. "They're headin' for the village."

Polly MacLug shook her head. This was more like a game of Wild West Cowboys. First, the pack had split. And now this - an 'ambush', for heaven's sake.

"Whip in those hounds on your side," she told her nephew crossly.

Smudge was too excited to listen. "YEEE-HAAAW," he roared, spurring his tired horse forward.

Polly shook her head again. "A pair of ninnyhammers for nephews," she said out loud. "If only you were half as smart as those foxes. They are two crafty animals. What will they think of next?"

15 Wild Goose Chase

Katie, Janet and Conor stood on the bridge at Clonowen, staring at the waterfall. It rushed with the speed of a train and crashed like thunder. They had never seen it like this before.

"I'd hate to fall in," shouted Janet over the boom of water.

Conor lifted his arms and made a face like a lion. "Listen to that R-R-R-ROAR-R-R-R!"

He picked up a stick and hurled it over the edge. "Geronimo!"

"Look," Katie suddenly called out.

Her friends turned, just in time to see a pair of foxes race by.

Katie, Conor and Janet dashed after them.

"Let's catch them," cried Conor.

Katie knew there was no chance of that.

Ash and Misty hurried down to the village square. It was broad daylight, but they did not care. They were on their last legs.

They passed the *Golden Boat Takeaway* and *The Horse and Hound Tavern*. A man sweeping the path stopped to look at them, as did the two ladies chatting outside *Nolan's Sweet Shop*. But the old Alsatian lying by the wall never noticed a thing. Then they turned the corner, where a red van was parked.

At this moment Raptor and Slicer arrived. Master and hound looked this way and that, unsure of which way to go.

"Have you seen the foxes, little girl?" Slicer asked Katie, who was outside the *Golden Boat Takeaway*.

"They went that way," said Katie pointing to Hillside Terrace.

Slicer's cold, blue eye peered down at her. "Are you sure little girl?"

"Sure."

Without even a 'thank you', Slicer trotted on.

"Tee-hee, I fooled him," said Katie to her friends.

"Oh, you told a lie," said Conor. "You'll get into trouble."

"I won't," said Katie. "My Mam and Dad like foxes. And they don't like the MacLugs."

"I won't tell on you," said Conor.

"I won't either," said Janet.

"Look," said Katie, her eyes widening. "Here's the rest of the hunt."

Down into the village came Polly, Smudge and the pack of tail-wagging foxhounds.

Janet giggled into her hands. "Katie, Katie, will you send them the wrong way too?" she whispered.

Katie's eyes sparkled mischievously.

Polly patted her horse and leaped from the saddle. "Okay, that's it for now," she said, giving Smudge a big grin.

"What d'you mean Auntie?"

"I think I'll call it a day - need a hot drink," she said, nodding towards *The Horse and Hound*. "Care to join me?"

"Ya can't do that Auntie Polly. What about them foxes?"

"Those foxes have given us a run for our money, Master Smudge. They deserve a break."

"We can't just let them go!"

"There'll be another day, another hunt."

"Well, I'm not givin' up, and Slicer won't either."

"Speak of the devil," said Polly. "Here he comes now."

Katie slipped into *Nolan's Sweet Shop* as Slicer rode back across the square.

"Some little brat sent me on a wild goose chase," he told them, scowling. "A fox lover, I suppose," he added in disgust. "Polly, don't tell me you're throwing in the towel?"

"No, Polly's putting the kettle on," his aunt replied, laughing.

"The bet's still on?" asked Slicer.

She grinned. "The money is yours if you catch even one of them."

"We will," said Slicer. He took a knife out of his pocket and held it up. "I'll bring you the brush to prove it."

"Now you're talkin', Boss," laughed Smudge. "We'll chop off their tails with a carvin' knife. You'll never see such a thing in your life!"

Polly MacLug shook her head. What a pair of nephews she had.

"Right, let's get a move on," said Slicer, lifting the reins.

"Hey, look," said Smudge, the smile vanishing from his face. "Raptor's on to somethin'."

Katie, who was watching from the shop, saw to her horror that the MacLugs' hound was heading for the corner.

In fact, he was heading for the RED VAN parked at the corner.

16 Cakes Galore!

Jody Eaton, son of the owner of Eaton's Cakes, closed the back door of his van. Jody was a smart, fresh-faced lad of eighteen who did not wear glasses. Perhaps he should have worn glasses, for how else could he have missed the pair of foxes lying on an empty cake-tray in the back?

Jody climbed into his van and drove off. Had he looked in the mirror, he might - or might not - have seen a large hound rounding the corner.

The hound was chasing his van.

"I think we're going somewhere," Ash whispered.

"I think we're trapped," said Misty.

"Don't worry. The minute he opens the door again, we pile out."

Misty gave her brother a look. "What got into your head to hide in here?"

"I'm sorry, Misty, I was exhausted. I saw the van and just jumped in."

"I know you like cakes but this is crazy," said his sister.

CAKES. The word brought Ash to his senses.

"Did you say 'cakes'?" he enquired. He shot a glance at the tray next to him and the eyes almost popped out of his head.

The tray was full of cakes.

"This cannot be happening," gasped Ash, his mouth starting to water.

Misty sat up. "I suppose we may as well help ourselves."

"You bet," said Ash.

They gazed at the cakes before them.

"Chocolate cake," whispered Ash.

"Cherry cake," whimpered Misty.

"Cream buns."

"And mince pies."

"Carrot cake."

"Hey, is that trifle?"

"Yeah."

"This is heaven."

"Which one are you going for first?"

"I think I'll start with a little mince pie - it's Christmas after all."

"I'm having the chocolate cake."

"But leave some for me."

"Heh, heh, I might leave you a crumb or two."

The two foxes fell upon the feast as the van rattled down the road.

17 Jingle Bells

Ash had moved on to the cream buns and Misty was attacking mince pies when the van came to a stop, at *Nelly's Coffee Shop* less than a half-mile outside the village.

"Oh dear," sighed Misty.

Then the engine switched off and they heard Jody singing:

Jingle Bells, Jingle Bells
Jingle all the way
Oh what fun it is to ride
On a one-horse open sleigh!

"What'll we do?" whispered Ash.

Misty swallowed a bit of mince pie and said nothing.

"Misty, I think I'm going to get sick," moaned Ash.

"Sh-sh-sh," she whispered.

The driver's door opened, and they heard the clump of boots on the gravel.

Dashing through the snow
On a one-horse open sleigh

Ash stared at Misty in terror.

"Hold your nerve," hissed Misty.

Clump, Clump, Clump, Clump came the sound of Jody's boots by the side of the van.

Misty's heart pounded. Ash began to retch.

O'er the fields we go
Laughing all the way
Ha ha ha!

Suddenly they heard another voice call out.

"You're in fine voice today, Jody."

"Mornin', Nelly."

"Have a good Christmas?"

"Had a grand time. And yourself?"

"Grand, grand. We'd a big run on the cakes though - ate most of them ourselves!"

"Good for you, Nelly. What can I give you?"

"The usual - five dozen buns and six of your best Eaton cakes."

"Mince pies?"

"Throw in a dozen. We'll keep the Christmas party going."

"That's the spirit, Nelly."

Jody Eaton's hands reached out and opened the back door of his van.

"What the-!"

Misty and Ash shot out like bullets.

They scurried back up the road, towards the bridge.

"The rascals!" cried Jody hurling a mince pie after them. Beside him, Nelly doubled up with laughter.

Then Jody started laughing too. "Look at the state of my van, Nellie..."

Misty stopped at the bridge when she saw they were not being chased. Ash had halted too, but for another reason.

"Ash, that is disgusting," said Misty as her brother threw up at the side of the road.

Feeling the better for it, Ash gave himself a shake and stretch. "Now I know how Dad felt after those spare ribs."

"I can't bring you anywhere, can I?" Misty snapped. "It's one thing after the other."

"Shame about all that chocolate cake, though," said her brother, "and the cream buns!"

"That is just SICK!" said Misty. "Can we get out of here please?"

"No problem. We'll head for-" Ash froze, staring at something on the bridge right behind his sister.

"What's up?" said Misty, whipping round.

She felt herself go weak when she saw who was there.

18 Raptor's Leap

Slicer was on horseback, with Smudge on foot holding Raptor on the lead.

The instant the hound saw the foxes, he lunged forward, pulling his master with him.

"Release him, man, release him," cried Slicer.

"I'm trying," bellowed Smudge.

He clamped his big hobnailed boots to the gravel and tugged with all his might. "Come here, you mutt."

"Hurry, man, hurry, they're getting away," screamed Slicer.

Finally, Smudge caught hold of the hound's collar and set him free.

With one bound the hound was over the ditch, into the field and after the foxes.

"Go on, Raptor, my boy," shouted Slicer.

"We have them at last," cheered Smudge, waving his big fists in the air.

Once again, Ash and Misty fled for their lives. This was the final throw of the dice and they knew it.

Side by side, the foxes ran up the muddy slope. Misty's strength drained like water from a sink. She felt the beast coming closer.

"He's catchin' them, he's catchin' them," roared Smudge as Raptor homed in on his target.

"Go on, boy, do it," urged Slicer.

Raptor was almost upon them. Misty swerved to her left and as she did a glimmer of something caught her eye.

THE RIVER.

Just then the beast lunged at her, sending her spinning.

She crashed into Ash, taking him down.

"YEE-HAW," roared Smudge.

"That's fifty big ones in my pocket," Slicer sang out.

But Raptor lost his grip and fell too.

Misty got to her feet in a flash.

So did Ash.

And so did Raptor.

"Get to the river!" Misty cried.

Raptor knew what they were up to. He had to get one of them if it was the last thing he did. With a great surge of power, he rushed to cut them off.

This time he set his sights on Ash.

He was too late.

SPLASH. Misty hit the water first.

Then came her brother. SPLASH.

And a micro-second later, with the biggest SPLASH of all, went Raptor, into the Clonowen River.

"Cowdung!" roared Smudge from the bridge. He threw his woollen cap on the ground and stamped on it with his dirty hobnailed boots.

19 Down the River

Misty felt the shock of water on her skin. The swirling river tossed her this way and that. She gasped for air and paddled furiously to stay afloat.

Her father's words echoed in her ears: "Water is a fox's best friend". It did not feel that way now.

Her head went down under the water. As she rose again, she saw Raptor being swept away ahead of her. Then, turning with the current, she spotted the bank jutting out.

I can get out of here, she thought.

But where was her brother?

"Ash," she called out.

"Over here," came Ash's cry above the noise of water.

Lifting her head, she caught a glimpse of him bobbing up and down. A second later he vanished.

"Hold on, I'm coming," she called and swam after him.

Then she, too, was carried away.

"Look, Boss, there's one of them," shouted Smudge, pointing down from the bridge.

Slicer leaned over, peering down at Misty as she swept past. "That's my money down the river."

Smudge ran to the other side of the bridge and bellowed after the fox: "You think you've won, but you haven't. Say goodbye, loser, Ha, ha, ha!"

The brothers watched the fox disappear around the bend in the river.

"Do you think they've got a chance?" wondered Smudge.

"Not a hope," said Slicer coldly.

"What about Raptor?"

"What about him?" answered Slicer with a shrug.

Down and away rushed the waters of the Clonowen River, past John's Wood...and Heron's Rock...past Little Island...and Wooden Bridge...past the Round Tower on the bend ... till at last the village of Clonowen came into view.

Now the white waters surged out of control.

Next, a deep thundering sound rose up from somewhere below - the awful sound of the Clonowen Falls.

Misty opened her eyes and took one last look at the sky as she went over the top.

She did not try to fight it. She just let herself go.
Down. Down. Down.

The free-fall ended with a mighty bang.

At once she was tossed like a sock in a washing machine. The roar was deafening. Not an inch could she see in the boiling water.

She held her breath and began to count:

One, two, three, four...

She kicked with her legs, trying to get some control, but it was no use. Round and round and upside down she went.

Ten, eleven, twelve, thirteen...

Still the waters crashed and churned.

Twenty, twenty-one, twenty-two...

She felt like she would burst. She could not hold on any longer.

Twenty-nine, thirty...

Just as she let go, something caught hold of her. Or rather, she felt herself being held - the way her mother once held her as a cub - by the back of Misty's neck, with her teeth, gently and safely.

Just as her mother had once lifted her from the ground, so Ash, her brother, dragged her from the water.

And as he did, she passed out.

20 A Discovery

"Misty, are you all right? Misty?"

She woke with a start at her brother's voice.

For a moment she thought she was in her den. Then she saw that she was stretched out on a rock, soaked to the skin. *What am I doing here?* she thought. Too weak to talk, she just smiled at him with her eyes.

"We made it, Misty. We're safe. Get up and look around."

She wondered why Ash was barking so excitedly. And what was that other awful noise?

"Get up and have a look, Misty. You'd never guess where we are."

Turning her head around, she saw the great white curtain of water crashing down in front of her.

"Now, I remember," she said.

But she was still puzzled. What had happened? Where was she?

She sat up, staring at the waterfall. It was some time before she spoke.

"Are we...are we inside it?" she asked. "Ash?"

Her brother was not there.

She stood up and shook the water from herself. "Ash," she called out. "Where are you?"

"Over here." Her brother came out of the shadows.

"Are we where I think we are?" she asked

"Yes."

"So we're inside the waterfall."

"Behind the waterfall," he corrected her.

"Then we're trapped."

"No, I think I've found a way out," said Ash, beaming.

"You are a genius," said Misty.

One step at a time, she followed him along a narrow ledge as the water thundered down on one side, and dripped and splashed from rock on the other.

Soon the ledge widened into a cave.

"Wait till you see this," said Ash.

They stepped inside.

"It's dry in here," said Misty. "It's not too dark either."

"I'll show you why it's not dark," said her brother. "Come with me."

The floor sloped upwards as they walked on and the walls narrowed into a tunnel. The walls glowed with a dim golden light.

They began to walk faster.

The tunnel turned sharply and they saw a tiny bright circle of light ahead.

"Hurray," they yelped.

They broke into a run.

"Hold it," cried Misty just as they reached the opening.

Ash stopped in his tracks. The light dazzled his

eyes.

"We don't want to go out there right now," she told him.

"You're right," said Ash. "Do you think that hound could still be around?"

"Don't worry about him. He's gone forever," said Misty.

"Well, let me have just one peep then," said Ash.

He crept up to the opening, which was the size of a pumpkin and as perfectly round, and stuck his head out.

He saw grass, trees and the blue, blue sky.

21 My Life, Your Life

They waited for the sun to go down.

The time flew for there was plenty to do in the cave. They discovered other tunnels running this way and that, tunnels so dark the foxes would only go a few steps inside. But it was a great place to play Hide and Seek.

After playing at least ten games, they went back to the waterfall for a drink. Then they walked further along the ledge - getting drenched again (but they didn't mind) - and here they discovered another room. This one had no way out.

On the floor, they found a pile of bones, big bones.

"I've never seen bones like these before, have you?" whispered Ash.

"How did they get in here?" wondered Misty.

"Let's see what they taste like."

Both foxes began to gnaw on the bones, but almost immediately dropped them.

"They taste bad," said Ash.

"They're old," said his sister. "Very old."

Misty was right (She didn't know it, but the bones belonged to a bear that had lived in the cave thousands of years ago.)

"I wonder what else we'll find?" said Ash.

"It's a great place. I can't wait to show Mam and Dad."

"Me too."

"We could all live here."

"That's a brilliant idea, Misty."

"It's warm and dry. And it's safe, not like the woods."

"No-one would ever find us in here, ever."

"And we could sneak out at night."

Ash's eyes lit up. "Yeah, and steal things from the MacLugs, starting with their chickens."

"Steady on now, steady on," said Misty. "The first thing we have to do is make our way home."

"You said it, Sister."

They went back to the tunnel. By now, the sun had gone down. The opening was a circle of gold mixed with red.

"Let's wait another bit," said Misty, "to be on the safe side."

They lay down, curling up together. A short while later, they began to snooze.

When they awoke, the circle was a velvety blue

framing two twinkling stars.

At last, Misty and Ash climbed out into the night. They stood for a moment gazing at the full moon that had risen above the trees.

"You saved my life today," said Misty, turning to her brother.

"And you saved mine," said Ash.

"And we both saved Mam's and Dad's lives," said Misty. She looked up at the moon again and added: "It's been some day."

22 Dreams

"I'd love a feed of chips," said Ash as they neared the village. "But not from that takeaway," he quickly added.

"Sh-sh-sh-h-h, we've got to be careful here," whispered Misty.

They had crossed the river by a small wooden bridge and were making their way along a dark road at the back of Hillside Terrace.

"I know those houses up there," said Ash.

Misty looked at the corner house. "That's where we got the biscuits, wasn't it?"

"Yeah, do you think they'll leave out more for us?"

"Sure they will - won't we be living close by?"

"We will, if Mam and Dad agree."

"They will," said Misty. "Now, let's get a move on."

Disappearing into the shadows, they headed up the steep hill towards Hillside Terrace and the village square.

Even though it was midnight, Katie was still awake, standing by her bedroom window. She had

tried counting sheep earlier, but had given up at number 103. The foxes were on her mind. She had heard what happened at *Nelly's Coffee Shop* (Jody Eaton had brought the story to the village and the news had spread like wildfire.)

Those poor foxes, I wonder if they drowned? she thought. *They're such brave little things. They don't harm anyone. They might steal a few chickens now and then, but everyone has to live. Why can't people just leave them alone?*

She closed her eyes, crossed her fingers (and her toes) and wished upon the two twinkling stars above the village church. "Please, please let me see them," she whispered.

When she opened her eyes, she saw that dreams do come true sometimes.

Ash and Misty saw her too. Crossing the square, they stopped for a moment as she waved from the window.

"That's our friend up there," said Ash.

"We'll visit her soon," said Misty.

Right now, though, they wanted to get back to their parents. So they hurried on.

23 Free at Last

Misty was wrong about one thing. Raptor was not gone.

He had survived the waterfall and the river that had swept him all the way down to the sea.

While the foxes made their way home he slept like a puppy, in the sand dunes on Clonowen Beach.

It was a long and refreshing sleep.

When he awoke, he was a new dog.

"I'll never go back to the MacLugs," he decided. "I'm not their hound. Or anyone else's hound. I'll not be locked up in a cage. Or beg for food. Ever again."

High above him, the moon shone, laying down a silvery path across the bay. Raptor had never felt so happy.

"I belong to me," he said. "And I am free."

Then, like a wolf, he began to howl.

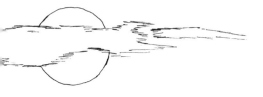

AVAILABLE BY POST

BRUSH
A Tale of Two Foxes

<u>ORDER FORM</u>

	Price*	No. of Copies
Ireland	€6	....
United Kingdom	£4.50	....
North America	US$8.00	....
Europe	€7	....
Australia	AUS$14	....

Price includes postage and packaging

NAME ....

ADDRESS ....

....

....

....

Payment enclosed .... *(please fill in amount)*

Please send cheque/euro giro/money order to:

PIXIE BOOKS
72 Cabra Park, Phibsboro, Dublin 7, Ireland.
e-mail: gseekamp@eircom.net